# The HOME Team
## Calgary Flames®

Written by Holly Preston
Illustrated by Val Lawton

Always Books Ltd.

# The Home Team: Calgary Flames®

Manufactured by Friesens Corporation in Altona, MB, Canada
October 2014
Job # 205837

Preston, Holly, author
The home team : Calgary Flames / written by Holly Preston ; illustrated by Val Lawton.

ISBN 978-0-9869244-9-1 (pbk.)

1. Calgary Flames (Hockey team)—Juvenile fiction.
I. Lawton, Val, 1962-, illustrator  II. Title.

PS8631.R467H6422 2014      jC813'.6      C2014-906374-1

Layout by Heather Nickel

MIX
Paper from
responsible sources
FSC® C016245

Always Books Ltd.
AFANFORLIFE.COM

In memory of Chad Gabora,
a young coach who instilled his love of the game
and his love for the FLAMES® in his young players.

There was nothing better than playing hockey …

… except watching hockey when the **CALGARY FLAMES** played.

Owen played defence. Logan played forward. Liam was in goal.
The boys played different positions. They had the same dream:
to one day play for the **CALGARY FLAMES**.

Even after playing all day, Logan dreamed only about hockey.

The only problem was Logan never scored. Ever.
The puck went high. The puck went low.
The puck went everywhere but where it was supposed to go.

*How can I ever become one of the* **CALGARY FLAMES**? Logan wondered.

His sister Avery was the best goal scorer in the neighbourhood.

"The **FLAMES** were little boys once, too, Logan," his dad said.
"They didn't become hockey stars overnight.

His mom said, "You can learn a lot by watching what the **FLAMES** do."
She'd been a **FLAMES** fan forever.

The **FLAMES** are great skaters.

They make big plays.

They shoot. They score!

And make a million saves.

"The only way to get better is to practise," said Owen.
And so they practised hard. And then came the best surprise they'd ever had.
"We're going to a **FLAMES** game!" Liam yelled.

But at the game, the **FLAMES'** top scorer wasn't scoring at all!
"Something is wrong," said Logan.

The next day on the way to the rink, Logan found a shiny chain.
He put it on and … he got a goal! And then another one!
"That's a good luck charm, for sure," Avery said.

"Our player lost his good luck charm, kids," said Dad. "Maybe *that's* why he hasn't been scoring." The children knew hockey players were superstitious. They also knew where that charm was ...

And what they had to do next!

Logan seized the moment.
"What does it take to play for the **CALGARY FLAMES**?" he asked.

Play like a team…

…and with heart.

Never give up.

Believe in yourself.

"The **FLAMES** are the greatest team in the NHL," said Owen.

"We're going to be **FLAMES** fans forever," added Liam.

Everything was the way it should be.

All the next week Logan practised and practised.
He no longer had the good luck charm, but he had something else—
he believed in himself.

And that was all he really needed.

But Logan, like all hockey players, knew a little luck always helps…

…especially when you're playing for the Stanley Cup®!

## ABOUT THE AUTHOR
# Holly Preston

*Holly Preston is a journalist who worked for CTV and CBC. She grew up watching NHL hockey with her brother and father. Now she creates children's picture books for professional sports teams. She hopes Flames fans will enjoy having a book that celebrates their home team and encourages young fans to find a love of reading.*

## ABOUT THE ILLUSTRATOR
# Val Lawton

*Val Lawton is an artist, an artist-educator with the Learning Through the Arts Program, and a children's book illustrator. The Home Team: Calgary Flames is her 29th book.*